STEVENSON SCHOOL
2106 ARROWHEAD DR.
BLOOMINGTON, IL 61704

STEVENSON LEARNING CENTER

Waking Beauty

Leah Wilcox

ILLUSTRATED BY
Lydia Monks

G. P. PUTNAM'S SONS

G. P. PUTNAM'S SONS
A division of Penguin Young Readers Group.
Published by The Penguin Group.
Penguin Group (USA) Inc., 375 Hudson Street, New York, NY 10014, U.S.A.
Penguin Group (Canada), 90 Eglinton Avenue East, Suite 700, Toronto, Ontario M4P 2Y3, Canada
(a division of Pearson Penguin Canada Inc.).
Penguin Books Ltd, 80 Strand, London WC2R 0RL, England.
Penguin Ireland, 25 St. Stephen's Green, Dublin 2, Ireland (a division of Penguin Books Ltd.).
Penguin Group (Australia), 250 Camberwell Road, Camberwell, Victoria 3124, Australia
(a division of Pearson Australia Group Pty Ltd).
Penguin Books India Pvt Ltd, 11 Community Centre, Panchsheel Park, New Delhi - 110 017, India.
Penguin Group (NZ), 67 Apollo Drive, Rosedale, North Shore 0745, Auckland, New Zealand
(a division of Pearson New Zealand Ltd.).
Penguin Books (South Africa) (Pty) Ltd, 24 Sturdee Avenue, Rosebank, Johannesburg 2196, South Africa.
Penguin Books Ltd, Registered Offices: 80 Strand, London WC2R 0RL, England.

Published simultaneously in Canada.
Manufactured in China by South China Printing Co. Ltd.
Design by Marikka Tamura. Text set in Greco Negra.
Library of Congress Cataloging-in-Publication Data
Wilcox, Leah. Waking Beauty / Leah Wilcox ; illustrated by Lydia Monks. p. cm.
Summary: Prince Charming tries all sorts of silly ways to wake Sleeping Beauty
before he learns how he is really supposed to wake her up.
[1. Characters in literature—Fiction. 2. Humorous stories. 3. Stories in rhyme.]
I. Monks, Lydia, ill. II. Title.
PZ8.3.W6587Wak 2008 [E]—dc22 2007007377
ISBN 978-0-399-24615-9
1 3 5 7 9 10 8 6 4 2

For my delightful daughters,
Chandler, Shaelia and Adrienne, who are beauties inside and out,
and for Chase, my valiant, charming, sometimes alarming son,
who holds his own in the midst of them. —L. W.

Once upon a Saturday,
in search of dragons he could slay,

Prince Charming heard a dreadful sound
that shook the land for miles around.

It thundered from a castle tall.
He raced to scale its prickly wall.

"A dragon lies within!" he cried,
and hand on sword, he crept inside . . .

then hung his head. "Oh, rats," he said,
"it's just a snoring girl in bed."

He peeked behind her canopy
and spied some fairies, one, two, three.

"She's snored this way one hundred years,"
they whimpered through their fairy tears.

"That long?" He frowned. "She sure sleeps late.
Wake her up! Why do you wait?"

The fairies scowled. "Don't be so dense.
She'll only wake up for a prince."

"We see you finally made the trip,
now give the girl a little lip."

"Okay," he said. "If you insist."
He drew his mouth up in a twist,

and hollered, "WAKE UP, LAZYBONES!"
Her snores drowned out the fairies' groans.

They shook their heads. "No, not like *this*,
you have to wake her with a—"

"Hey! I know!" He tapped his head
and started jumping on the bed.

Beauty shot up, hoops and all,
then sailed down like a parasol.

This did not wake the maiden fair
but loosed the cobwebs in her hair.

The fairies all began to hiss,
"She'll only wake to True Love's—"

"Wait!" Prince Charming waved his hand.
"Don't worry, girls, I understand."

And stooping o'er her snoring snout,
he dumped a water pitcher out.

On she slept, she did not stir.
Thick dust had turned to mud on her.

The feisty fairies grabbed his ear,
making certain he could hear.

"Take careful aim, you *must not miss!*
You have to wake her with a—"

"Ohhh, I know what you were plannin'."
Prince Charming spied a castle cannon.

He stuffed the sleeping Beauty in. . . .

She soon came shooting out again.

Ka~Boom!
She fell into the moat,
where all her hoops
kept her afloat.

Still, on she snored as frightened trout
and crocodiles jumped right out.

Prince Charming fished the girl ashore.
The fairies yelled, "ENOUGH! NO MORE!"

They fluttered 'round him, feeling frantic.
"How *can* you be so unromantic?"

"She won't have ever-after bliss
until you wake her with a

The Prince's knees began to shake.
His noble heart began to quake.

"One hundred years of morning breath.
Wow! That could be the kiss of death!"

He poked her muddy, matted curls.
"I've heard that there are *germs* on girls."

He wiped her mouth clean with his shirt.
"I hope," he squeaked, "this doesn't hurt. . . ."

His puckered lips
met Beauty's: SMACK!
And in her sleep
she kissed him back.

Prince Charming smiled. "Not bad," he said.
The maiden sat up in her bed.

She stretched and yawned and rubbed her eyes.
Then, much to everyone's surprise,

she popped Prince Charming with her fist.
"Who said that you could have a kiss?"

The pummeled Prince slid down, poor chap,
and fell asleep on Beauty's lap.

Beauty groaned and bent to shake him.
"Fairies, tell me how to wake him!"

"Just let the poor boy sleep," they said.
And, tired too, they went to bed.

But fairy tales can't end like this,
we know she woke him with a . . .